A FAINT HEART

BY

FYODOR DOSTOEVSKY

FROM THE RUSSIAN BY

CONSTANCE GARNETT

British Library Cataloguing-in-Publication Data
A catalogue record for this book is available
from the British Library

CONTENTS

FYODOR DOSTOEVSKY

Fyodor Mikhailovich Dostoevsky was born in Moscow, as the second son of a former army doctor. Raised within the grounds of the Mariinsky hospital, at an early age he was introduced to English, French, German and Russian literature, as well as to fairy-tales and legends. He was educated at home and at a private school, but shortly after the death of his mother in 1837, he was sent to St. Petersburg, where he entered the Army Engineering College.

In 1839 Dostoevsky's father died. A year later, Dostoevsky graduated as a military engineer, but resigned in 1844 to devote himself to writing. While earning money from translations, he wrote his first novel, *Poor Folk,* which appeared in 1846. It was followed by *The Double* (1846), which depicted a man who was haunted by a look-alike who eventually usurps his position.

In 1846, Dostoevsky joined a group of utopian socialists. He was arrested in 1849 and sentenced to death. After a mock execution, his sentence was reduced to imprisonment in Siberia. Dostoevsky spent four years in hard labour – ten years later, he would turn these experiences into *The House of the Dead* (1860). Upon his release, he joined the army in Semipalatinsk (North-East Kazakhstan), where he remained for a further four years.

Dostoevsky returned to St. Petersburg in 1854. Three years later, he married Maria Isaev, a 29-year old widow. He resigned from the army in 1859, and focussed once more on writing. Between the years 1861 and 1863 he served as editor of the monthly periodical *Time*, which was later suppressed because of an article on the Polish uprising.

In 1864-65 his wife and brother died and Dostoevsky was burdened with debts. The situation was made worse by his own lifelong gambling addiction. From the turmoil of the 1860s emerged his classic *Notes from the Underground* (1864), a psychological study of a social outcast seeking spiritual rebirth. The novel marked a watershed in Dostoevsky's artistic development.

Notes from the Underground (1864) was followed by Dostoevsky's most famous work, *Crime and Punishment* (1866). An account of an individual's fall and redemption, and an implicit critique of nihilism, it is now regarded as one of the greatest works of Russian literature. Two years later *The Idiot* (1868) was published, and three years after that came *The Possessed*, (1871) an exploration of philosophical nihilism.

In 1867 Dostoevsky married Anna Snitkin, his 22-year old stenographer. They travelled abroad and returned in 1871. By the time the *The Brothers Karamazov* was published, between 1879-80, Dostoevsky was recognized in his own country as one of its great writers. However, having suffered from a fragile mental disposition his whole life, Dostoevsky began to succumb to larger periods of mania and rage. After a particularly bad epileptic fit, he died in St. Petersburg in early 1881, aged 59.

Together with Leo Tolstoy, Dostoevsky is now regarded as one of the greatest and most influential novelists in all of Russian literature. His books have been translated into more than 170 languages and have sold around 15 million copies.

A FAINT HEART

A Story

Under the same roof in the same flat on the same fourth
storey lived two young men, colleagues in the service, Arkady
Ivanovitch Nefedevitch and Vasya Shumkov.... The author of
course, feels the necessity of explaining to the reader why one is
given his full title, while the other's name is abbreviated, if only
that such a mode of expression may not be regarded as unseemly
and rather familiar. But, to do so, it would first be necessary to
explain and describe the rank and years and calling and duty
in the service, and even, indeed, the characters of the persons
concerned; and since there are so many writers who begin in that
way, the author of the proposed story, solely in order to be unlike
them (that is, some people will perhaps say, entirely on account of
his boundless vanity), decides to begin straightaway with action.
Having completed this introduction, he begins.

Towards six o'clock on New Year's Eve Shumkov returned
home. Arkady Ivanovitch, who was lying on the bed, woke up
and looked at his friend with half-closed eyes. He saw that Vasya
had on his very best trousers and a very clean shirt front. That,
of course, struck him. "Where had Vasya to go like that? And he
had not dined at home either!" Meanwhile, Shumkov had lighted
a candle, and Arkady Ivanovitch guessed immediately that his
friend was intending to wake him accidentally. Vasya did, in
fact, clear his throat twice, walked twice up and down the room,
and at last, quite accidentally, let the pipe, which he had begun
filling in the corner by the stove, slip out of his hands. Arkady
Ivanovitch laughed to himself.

"Vasya, give over pretending!" he said.

"Arkasha, you are not asleep?"

"I really cannot say for certain; it seems to me I am not."

"Oh, Arkasha! How are you, dear boy? Well, brother! Well, brother!... You don't know what I have to tell you!"

"I certainly don't know; come here."

As though expecting this, Vasya went up to him at once, not at all anticipating, however, treachery from Arkady Ivanovitch. The other seized him very adroitly by the arms, turned him over, held him down, and began, as it is called, "strangling" his victim, and apparently this proceeding afforded the lighthearted Arkady Ivanovitch great satisfaction.

"Caught!" he cried. "Caught!"

"Arkasha, Arkasha, what are you about? Let me go. For goodness sake, let me go, I shall crumple my dress coat!"

"As though that mattered! What do you want with a dress coat? Why were you so confiding as to put yourself in my hands? Tell me, where have you been? Where have you dined?"

"Arkasha, for goodness sake, let me go!"

"Where have you dined?"

"Why, it's about that I want to tell you."

"Tell away, then."

"But first let me go."

"Not a bit of it, I won't let you go till you tell me!"

"Arkasha! Arkasha! But do you understand, I can't—it is utterly impossible!" cried Vasya, helplessly wriggling out of his friend's powerful clutches, "you know there are subjects!"

"How—subjects?"...

"Why, subjects that you can't talk about in such a position without losing your dignity; it's utterly impossible; it would make it ridiculous, and this is not a ridiculous matter, it is important."

"Here, he's going in for being important! That's a new idea! You tell me so as to make me laugh, that's how you must tell me; I don't want anything important; or else you are no true friend of mine. Do you call yourself a friend? Eh?"

"Arkasha, I really can't!"

"Well, I don't want to hear...."

"Well, Arkasha!" began Vasya, lying across the bed and doing his utmost to put all the dignity possible into his words. "Arkasha! If you like, I will tell you; only...."

"Well, what?..."

"Well, I am engaged to be married!"

Without uttering another word Arkady Ivanovitch took Vasya up in his arms like a baby, though the latter was by no means short, but rather long and thin, and began dexterously carrying him up and down the room, pretending that he was hushing him to sleep.

"I'll put you in your swaddling clothes, Master Bridegroom," he kept saying. But seeing that Vasya lay in his arms, not stirring or uttering a word, he thought better of it at once, and reflecting that the joke had gone too far, set him down in the middle of the room and kissed him on the cheek in the most genuine and friendly way.

"Vasya, you are not angry?"

"Arkasha, listen...."

"Come, it's New Year's Eve."

"Oh, I'm all right; but why are you such a madman, such a scatterbrain? How many times I have told you: Arkasha, it's really not funny, not funny at all!"

"Oh, well, you are not angry?"

"Oh, I'm all right; am I ever angry with any one! But you have wounded me, do you understand?"

"But how have I wounded you? In what way?"

"I come to you as to a friend, with a full heart, to pour out my soul to you, to tell you of my happiness...."

"What happiness? Why don't you speak?..."

"Oh, well, I am going to get married!" Vasya answered with vexation, for he really was a little exasperated.

"You! You are going to get married! So you really mean it?" Arkasha cried at the top of his voice. "No, no ... but what's this? He talks like this and his tears are flowing.... Vasya, my little Vasya,

9

don't, my little son! Is it true, really?" And Arkady Ivanovitch flew to hug him again.

"Well, do you see, how it is now?" said Vasya. "You are kind, of course, you are a friend, I know that. I come to you with such joy, such rapture, and all of a sudden I have to disclose all the joy of my heart, all my rapture struggling across the bed, in an undignified way.... You understand, Arkasha," Vasya went on, half laughing. "You see, it made it seem comic: and in a sense I did not belong to myself at that minute. I could not let this be slighted.... What's more, if you had asked me her name, I swear, I would sooner you killed me than have answered you."

"But, Vasya, why did you not speak! You should have told me all about it sooner and I would not have played the fool!" cried Arkady Ivanovitch in genuine despair.

"Come, that's enough, that's enough! Of course, that's how it is.... You know what it all comes from—from my having a good heart. What vexes me is, that I could not tell you as I wanted to, making you glad and happy, telling you nicely and initiating you into my secret properly.... Really, Arkasha, I love you so much that I believe if it were not for you I shouldn't be getting married, and, in fact, I shouldn't be living in this world at all!"

Arkady Ivanovitch, who was excessively sentimental, cried and laughed at once as he listened to Vasya. Vasya did the same. Both flew to embrace one another again and forgot the past.

"How is it—how is it? Tell me all about it, Vasya! I am astonished, excuse me, brother, but I am utterly astonished; it's a perfect thunderbolt, by Jove! Nonsense, nonsense, brother, you have made it up, you've really made it up, you are telling fibs!" cried Arkady Ivanovitch, and he actually looked into Vasya's face with genuine uncertainty, but seeing in it the radiant confirmation of a positive intention of being married as soon as possible, threw himself on the bed and began rolling from side to side in ecstasy till the walls shook.

"Vasya, sit here," he said at last, sitting down on the bed.

"I really don't know, brother, where to begin!"

They looked at one another in joyful excitement.

"Who is she, Vasya?"

"The Artemyevs!..." Vasya pronounced, in a voice weak with emotion.

"No?"

"Well, I did buzz into your ears about them at first, and then I shut up, and you noticed nothing. Ah, Arkasha, if you knew how hard it was to keep it from you; but I was afraid, afraid to speak! I thought it would all go wrong, and you know I was in love, Arkasha! My God! my God! You see this was the trouble," he began, pausing continually from agitation, "she had a suitor a year ago, but he was suddenly ordered somewhere; I knew him—he was a fellow, bless him! Well, he did not write at all, he simply vanished. They waited and waited, wondering what it meant.... Four months ago he suddenly came back married, and has never set foot within their doors! It was coarse—shabby! And they had no one to stand up for them. She cried and cried, poor girl, and I fell in love with her ... indeed, I had been in love with her long before, all the time! I began comforting her, and was always going there.... Well, and I really don't know how it has all come about, only she came to love me; a week ago I could not restrain myself, I cried, I sobbed, and told her everything—well, that I love her—everything, in fact!... 'I am ready to love you, too, Vassily Petrovitch, only I am a poor girl, don't make a mock of me; I don't dare to love any one.' Well, brother, you understand! You understand?... On that we got engaged on the spot. I kept thinking and thinking and thinking and thinking, I said to her, 'How are we to tell your mother?' She said, 'It will be hard, wait a little; she's afraid, and now maybe she would not let you have me; she keeps crying, too.' Without telling her I blurted it out to her mother to-day. Lizanka fell on her knees before her, I did the same ... well, she gave us her blessing. Arkasha, Arkasha! My dear fellow! We will live together. No, I won't part from you for anything."

"Vasya, look at you as I may, I can't believe it. I don't believe it, I swear. I keep feeling as though.... Listen, how can you be engaged to be married?... How is it I didn't know, eh? Do you know, Vasya, I will confess it to you now. I was thinking of getting married myself; but now since you are going to be married, it is just as good! Be happy, be happy!..."

"Brother, I feel so lighthearted now, there is such sweetness in my soul ..." said Vasya, getting up and pacing about the room excitedly. "Don't you feel the same? We shall be poor, of course, but we shall be happy; and you know it is not a wild fancy; our happiness is not a fairy tale; we shall be happy in reality!..."

"Vasya, Vasya, listen!"

"What?" said Vasya, standing before Arkady Ivanovitch.

"The idea occurs to me; I am really afraid to say it to you.... Forgive me, and settle my doubts. What are you going to live on? You know I am delighted that you are going to be married, of course, I am delighted, and I don't know what to do with myself, but—what are you going to live on? Eh?"

"Oh, good Heavens! What a fellow you are, Arkasha!" said Vasya, looking at Nefedevitch in profound astonishment. "What do you mean? Even her old mother, even she did not think of that for two minutes when I put it all clearly before her. You had better ask what they are living on! They have five hundred roubles a year between the three of them: the pension, which is all they have, since the father died. She and her old mother and her little brother, whose schooling is paid for out of that income too—that is how they live! It's you and I are the capitalists! Some good years it works out to as much as seven hundred for me."

"I say, Vasya, excuse me; I really ... you know I ... I am only thinking how to prevent things going wrong. How do you mean, seven hundred? It's only three hundred...."

"Three hundred!... And Yulian Mastakovitch? Have you forgotten him?"

"Yulian Mastakovitch? But you know that's uncertain, brother; that's not the same thing as three hundred roubles of secure salary, where every rouble is a friend you can trust. Yulian

Mastakovitch, of course, he's a great man, in fact, I respect him, I understand him, though he is so far above us; and, by Jove, I love him, because he likes you and gives you something for your work, though he might not pay you, but simply order a clerk to work for him—but you will agree, Vasya.... Let me tell you, too, I am not talking nonsense. I admit in all Petersburg you won't find a handwriting like your handwriting, I am ready to allow that to you," Nefedevitch concluded, not without enthusiasm. "But, God forbid! you may displease him all at once, you may not satisfy him, your work with him may stop, he may take another clerk—all sorts of things may happen, in fact! You know, Yulian Mastakovitch may be here to-day and gone to-morrow...."

"Well, Arkasha, the ceiling might fall on our heads this minute."

"Oh, of course, of course, I mean nothing."

"But listen, hear what I have got to say—you know, I don't see how he can part with me.... No, hear what I have to say! hear what I have to say! You see, I perform all my duties punctually; you know how kind he is, you know, Arkasha, he gave me fifty roubles in silver to-day!"

"Did he really, Vasya? A bonus for you?"

"Bonus, indeed, it was out of his own pocket. He said: 'Why, you have had no money for five months, brother, take some if you want it; thank you, I am satisfied with you.'... Yes, really! 'Yes, you don't work for me for nothing,' said he. He did, indeed, that's what he said. It brought tears into my eyes, Arkasha. Good Heavens, yes!"

"I say, Vasya, have you finished copying those papers?..."

"No.... I haven't finished them yet."

"Vas...ya! My angel! What have you been doing?"

"Listen, Arkasha, it doesn't matter, they are not wanted for another two days, I have time enough...."

"How is it you have not done them?"

"That's all right, that's all right. You look so horror-stricken that you turn me inside out and make my heart ache! You are always going on at me like this! He's for ever crying out: Oh, oh, oh!!! Only consider, what does it matter? Why, I shall finish it, of course I shall finish it...."

"What if you don't finish it?" cried Arkady, jumping up, "and he has made you a present to-day! And you going to be married.... Tut, tut, tut!..."

"It's all right, it's all right," cried Shumkov, "I shall sit down directly, I shall sit down this minute."

"How did you come to leave it, Vasya?"

"Oh, Arkasha! How could I sit down to work! Have I been in a fit state? Why, even at the office I could scarcely sit still, I could scarcely bear the beating of my heart.... Oh! oh! Now I shall work all night, and I shall work all to-morrow night, and the night after, too—and I shall finish it."

"Is there a great deal left?"

"Don't hinder me, for goodness' sake, don't hinder me; hold your tongue."

Arkady Ivanovitch went on tip-toe to the bed and sat down, then suddenly wanted to get up, but was obliged to sit down again, remembering that he might interrupt him, though he could not sit still for excitement: it was evident that the news had thoroughly upset him, and the first thrill of delight had not yet passed off. He glanced at Shumkov; the latter glanced at him, smiled, and shook his finger at him, then, frowning severely (as though all his energy and the success of his work depended upon it), fixed his eyes on the papers.

It seemed that he, too, could not yet master his emotion; he kept changing his pen, fidgeting in his chair, re-arranging things, and setting to work again, but his hand trembled and refused to move.

"Arkasha, I've talked to them about you," he cried suddenly, as though he had just remembered it.

"Yes," cried Arkasha, "I was just wanting to ask you that. Well?"

"Well, I'll tell you everything afterwards. Of course, it is my own fault, but it quite went out of my head that I didn't mean to say anything till I had written four pages, but I thought of you and of them. I really can't write, brother, I keep thinking about you...."

Vasya smiled.

A silence followed.

"Phew! What a horrid pen," cried Shumkov, flinging it on the table in vexation. He took another.

"Vasya! listen! one word...."

"Well, make haste, and for the last time."

"Have you a great deal left to do?"

"Ah, brother!" Vasya frowned, as though there could be nothing more terrible and murderous in the whole world than such a question. "A lot, a fearful lot."

"Do you know, I have an idea——"

"What?"

"Oh, never mind, never mind; go on writing."

"Why, what? what?"

"It's past six, Vasya."

Here Nefedevitch smiled and winked slyly at Vasya, though with a certain timidity, not knowing how Vasya would take it.

"Well, what is it?" said Vasya, throwing down his pen, looking him straight in the face and actually turning pale with excitement.

"Do you know what?"

"For goodness sake, what is it?"

"I tell you what, you are excited, you won't get much done.... Stop, stop, stop! I have it, I have it—listen," said Nefedevitch, jumping up from the bed in delight, preventing Vasya from speaking and doing his utmost to ward off all objections; "first of all you must get calm, you must pull yourself together, mustn't you?"

"Arkasha, Arkasha!" cried Vasya, jumping up from his chair, "I will work all night, I will, really."

"Of course, of course, you won't go to bed till morning."

"I won't go to bed, I won't go to bed at all."

"No, that won't do, that won't do: you must sleep, go to bed at five. I will call you at eight. To-morrow is a holiday; you can sit and scribble away all day long.... Then the night and—but have you a great deal left to do?"

"Yes, look, look!"

Vasya, quivering with excitement and suspense, showed the manuscript: "Look!"

"I say, brother, that's not much."

"My dear fellow, there's some more of it," said Vasya, looking very timidly at Nefedevitch, as though the decision whether he was to go or not depended upon the latter.

"How much?"

"Two signatures."

"Well, what's that? Come, I tell you what. We shall have time to finish it, by Jove, we shall!"

"Arkasha!"

"Vasya, listen! To-night, on New Year's Eve, every one is at home with his family. You and I are the only ones without a home or relations.... Oh, Vasya!"

Nefedevitch clutched Vasya and hugged him in his leonine arms.

"Arkasha, it's settled."

"Vasya, boy, I only wanted to say this. You see, Vasya—listen, bandy-legs, listen!..."

Arkady stopped, with his mouth open, because he could not speak for delight. Vasya held him by the shoulders, gazed into his face and moved his lips, as though he wanted to speak for him.

"Well," he brought out at last.

"Introduce me to them to-day."

"Arkady, let us go to tea there. I tell you what, I tell you what. We won't even stay to see in the New Year, we'll come away earlier," cried Vasya, with genuine inspiration.

"That is, we'll go for two hours, neither more nor less...."

"And then separation till I have finished...."

"Vasya, boy!"

"Arkady!"

Three minutes later Arkady was dressed in his best. Vasya did nothing but brush himself, because he had been in such haste to work that he had not changed his trousers.

They hurried out into the street, each more pleased than the other. Their way lay from the Petersburg Side to Kolomna. Arkady Ivanovitch stepped out boldly and vigorously, so that from his walk alone one could see how glad he was at the good fortune of his friend, who was more and more radiant with happiness. Vasya trotted along with shorter steps, though his deportment was none the less dignified. Arkady Ivanovitch, in fact, had never seen him before to such advantage. At that moment he actually felt more respect for him, and Vasya's physical defect, of which the reader is not yet aware (Vasya was slightly deformed), which always called forth a feeling of loving sympathy in Arkady Ivanovitch's kind heart, contributed to the deep tenderness the latter felt for him at this moment, a tenderness of which Vasya was in every way worthy. Arkady Ivanovitch felt ready to weep with happiness, but he restrained himself.

"Where are you going, where are you going, Vasya? It is nearer this way," he cried, seeing that Vasya was making in the direction of Voznesenky.

"Hold your tongue, Arkasha."

"It really is nearer, Vasya."

"Do you know what, Arkasha?" Vasya began mysteriously, in a voice quivering with joy, "I tell you what, I want to take Lizanka a little present."

"What sort of present?"

"At the corner here, brother, is Madame Leroux's, a wonderful shop."

"Well."

"A cap, my dear, a cap; I saw such a charming little cap to-day. I inquired, I was told it was the *façon Manon Lescaut*—a delightful thing. Cherry-coloured ribbons, and if it is not dear ... Arkasha, even if it is dear...."

"I think you are superior to any of the poets, Vasya. Come along."

They ran along, and two minutes later went into the shop. They were met by a black-eyed Frenchwoman with curls, who, from the first glance at her customers, became as joyous and happy as they, even happier, if one may say so. Vasya was ready to kiss

Madame Leroux in his delight....

"Arkasha," he said in an undertone, casting a casual glance at all the grand and beautiful things on little wooden stands on the huge table, "lovely things! What's that? What's this? This one, for instance, this little sweet, do you see?" Vasya whispered, pointing to a charming cap further away, which was not the one he meant to buy, because he had already from afar descried and fixed his eyes upon the real, famous one, standing at the other end. He looked at it in such a way that one might have supposed some one was going to steal it, or as though the cap itself might take wings and fly into the air just to prevent Vasya from obtaining it.

"Look," said Arkady Ivanovitch, pointing to one, "I think that's better."

"Well, Arkasha, that does you credit; I begin to respect you for your taste," said Vasya, resorting to cunning with Arkasha in the tenderness of his heart, "your cap is charming, but come this way."

"Where is there a better one, brother?"

"Look; this way."

"That," said Arkady, doubtfully.

But when Vasya, incapable of restraining himself any longer, took it from the stand from which it seemed to fly spontaneously, as though delighted at falling at last into the hands of so good a customer, and they heard the rustle of its ribbons, ruches and lace, an unexpected cry of delight broke from the powerful chest of Arkady Ivanovitch. Even Madame Leroux, while maintaining her incontestable dignity and pre-eminence in matters of taste, and remaining mute from condescension, rewarded Vasya with a smile of complete approbation, everything in her glance, gesture and smile saying at once: "Yes, you have chosen rightly, and are worthy of the happiness which awaits you."

"It has been dangling its charms in coy seclusion," cried Vasya, transferring his tender feelings to the charming cap. "You have been hiding on purpose, you sly little pet!" And he kissed it, that is the air surrounding it, for he was afraid to touch his treasure.

"Retiring as true worth and virtue," Arkady added enthusiastically, quoting humorously from a comic paper he had read that morning. "Well, Vasya?"

"Hurrah, Arkasha! You are witty to-day. I predict you will make a sensation, as women say. Madame Leroux, Madame Leroux!"

"What is your pleasure?"

"Dear Madame Leroux."

Madame Leroux looked at Arkady Ivanovitch and smiled condescendingly.

"You wouldn't believe how I adore you at this moment.... Allow me to give you a kiss...." And Vasya kissed the shopkeeper.

She certainly at that moment needed all her dignity to maintain her position with such a madcap. But I contend that the innate, spontaneous courtesy and grace with which Madame Leroux received Vasya's enthusiasm, was equally befitting. She forgave him, and how tactfully, how graciously, she knew how to behave in the circumstances. How could she have been angry with Vasya?

"Madame Leroux, how much?"

"Five roubles in silver," she answered, straightening herself with a new smile.

"And this one, Madame Leroux?" said Arkady Ivanovitch, pointing to his choice.

"That one is eight roubles."

"There, you see—there, you see! Come, Madame Leroux, tell me which is nicer, more graceful, more charming, which of them suits you best?"

"The second is richer, but your choice *c'est plus coquet*."

"Then we will take it."

Madame Leroux took a sheet of very delicate paper, pinned it up, and the paper with the cap wrapped in it seemed even lighter than the paper alone. Vasya took it carefully, almost holding his breath, bowed to Madame Leroux, said something else very polite to her and left the shop.

"I am a lady's man, I was born to be a lady's man," said Vasya, laughing a little noiseless, nervous laugh and dodging the passers-by, whom he suspected of designs for crushing his precious cap.

"Listen, Arkady, brother," he began a minute later, and there was a note of triumph, of infinite affection in his voice. "Arkady, I am so happy, I am so happy!"

"Vasya! how glad I am, dear boy!"

"No, Arkasha, no. I know that there is no limit to your affection for me; but you cannot be feeling one-hundredth part of what I am feeling at this moment. My heart is so full, so full! Arkasha, I am not worthy of such happiness. I feel that, I am conscious of it. Why has it come to me?" he said, his voice full of stifled sobs. "What have I done to deserve it? Tell me. Look what lots of people, what lots of tears, what sorrow, what work-a-day life without a holiday, while I, I am loved by a girl like that, I.... But you will see her yourself immediately, you will appreciate her noble heart. I was born in a humble station, now I have a grade in the service and an independent income—my salary. I was born with a physical defect, I am a little deformed. See, she loves me as I am. Yulian Mastakovitch was so kind, so attentive, so gracious to-day; he does not often talk to me; he came up to me: 'Well, how goes it, Vasya' (yes, really, he called me Vasya), 'are you going to have a good time for the holiday, eh?' he laughed.

"'Well, the fact is, Your Excellency, I have work to do,' but then I plucked up courage and said: 'and maybe I shall have a good time, too, Your Excellency.' I really said it. He gave me the money, on the spot, then he said a couple of words more to me. Tears came into my eyes, brother, I actually cried, and he, too, seemed touched, he patted me on the shoulder, and said: 'Feel always, Vasya, as you feel this now.'"

Vasya paused for an instant. Arkady Ivanovitch turned away, and he, too, wiped away a tear with his fist.

"And, and ..." Vasya went on, "I have never spoken to you of this, Arkady.... Arkady, you make me so happy with your affection, without you I could not live,—no, no, don't say anything, Arkady, let me squeeze your hand, let me ... tha...ank ... you...." Again

20

Vasya could not finish.

Arkady Ivanovitch longed to throw himself on Vasya's neck, but as they were crossing the road and heard almost in their ears a shrill: "Hi! there!" they ran frightened and excited to the pavement.

Arkady Ivanovitch was positively relieved. He set down Vasya's outburst of gratitude to the exceptional circumstances of the moment. He was vexed. He felt that he had done so little for Vasya hitherto. He felt actually ashamed of himself when Vasya began thanking him for so little. But they had all their lives before them, and Arkady Ivanovitch breathed more freely.

The Artemyevs had quite given up expecting them. The proof of it was that they had already sat down to tea! And the old, it seems, are sometimes more clear-sighted than the young, even when the young are so exceptional. Lizanka had very earnestly maintained, "He isn't coming, he isn't coming, Mamma; I feel in my heart he is not coming;" while her mother on the contrary declared "that she had a feeling that he would certainly come, that he would not stay away, that he would run round, that he could have no office work now, on New Year's Eve." Even as Lizanka opened the door she did not in the least expect to see them, and greeted them breathlessly, with her heart throbbing like a captured bird's, flushing and turning as red as a cherry, a fruit which she wonderfully resembled. Good Heavens, what a surprise it was! What a joyful "Oh!" broke from her lips. "Deceiver! My darling!" she cried, throwing her arms round Vasya's neck. But imagine her amazement, her sudden confusion: just behind Vasya, as though trying to hide behind his back, stood Arkady Ivanovitch, a trifle out of countenance. It must be admitted that he was awkward in the company of women, very awkward indeed, in fact on one occasion something occurred ... but of that later. You must put yourself in his place, however. There was nothing to laugh at; he was standing in the entry, in his goloshes and overcoat, and in a cap with flaps over the ears, which he would have hastened to pull off, but he had, all twisted round in a hideous way, a yellow knitted scarf, which, to make things worse, was knotted at the back. He had to disentangle all this, to take it off as quickly as possible, to show himself to more advantage, for there is no one who does not prefer to show himself to advantage. And then Vasya, vexatious insufferable Vasya, of course always the same dear kind Vasya, but now insufferable, ruthless Vasya. "Here," he shouted, "Lizanka, I have brought you my Arkady? What do you think of him? He is my best friend, embrace him, kiss him, Lizanka, give him a kiss in advance; afterwards—you will know him better—you can take it back again."

Well, what, I ask you, was Arkady Ivanovitch to do? And he had only untwisted half of the scarf so far. I really am sometimes ashamed of Vasya's excess of enthusiasm; it is, of course, the sign of a good heart, but ... it's awkward, not nice!

At last both went in.... The mother was unutterably delighted to make Arkady Ivanovitch's acquaintance, "she had heard so much about him, she had...." But she did not finish. A joyful "Oh!" ringing musically through the room interrupted her in the middle of a sentence. Good Heavens! Lizanka was standing before the cap which had suddenly been unfolded before her gaze; she clasped her hands with the utmost simplicity, smiling such a smile.... Oh, Heavens! why had not Madame Leroux an even lovelier cap?

Oh, Heavens! but where could you find a lovelier cap? It was quite first-rate. Where could you get a better one? I mean it seriously. This ingratitude on the part of lovers moves me, in fact, to indignation and even wounds me a little. Why, look at it for yourself, reader, look, what could be more beautiful than this little love of a cap? Come, look at it.... But, no, no, my strictures are uncalled for; they had by now all agreed with me; it had been a momentary aberration; the blindness, the delirium of feeling; I am ready to forgive them.... But then you must look.... You must excuse me, kind reader, I am still talking about the cap: made of tulle, light as a feather, a broad cherry-coloured ribbon covered with lace passing between the tulle and the ruche, and at the back two wide long ribbons—they would fall down a little below the nape of the neck.... All that the cap needed was to be tilted a little to the back of the head; come, look at it; I ask you, after that ... but I see you are not looking ... you think it does not matter. You are looking in a different direction.... You are looking at two big tears, big as pearls, that rose in two jet black eyes, quivered for one instant on the eyelashes, and then dropped on the ethereal tulle of which Madame Leroux's artistic masterpiece was composed.... And again I feel vexed, those two tears were scarcely a tribute to the cap.... No, to my mind, such a gift should be given in cool blood, as only then can its full worth be appreciated. I am, I confess, dear reader, entirely on the side of the cap.

They sat down—Vasya with Lizanka and the old mother with Arkady Ivanovitch; they began to talk, and Arkady Ivanovitch did himself credit, I am glad to say that for him. One would hardly, indeed, have expected it of him. After a couple of words about Vasya he most successfully turned the conversation to Yulian Mastakovitch, his patron. And he talked so cleverly, so cleverly that the subject was not exhausted for an hour. You ought to have seen with what dexterity, what tact, Arkady Ivanovitch touched upon certain peculiarities of Yulian Mastakovitch which directly or indirectly affected Vasya. The mother was fascinated, genuinely fascinated; she admitted it herself; she purposely called Vasya aside, and said to him that his friend was a most excellent and charming young man, and, what was of most account, such a serious, steady young man. Vasya almost laughed aloud with delight. He remembered how the serious Arkady had tumbled him on his bed for a quarter of an hour. Then the mother signed to Vasya to follow her quietly and cautiously into the next room. It must be admitted that she treated Lizanka rather unfairly: she behaved treacherously to her daughter, in the fullness of her heart, of course, and showed Vasya on the sly the present Lizanka was preparing to give him for the New Year. It was a paper-case, embroidered in beads and gold in a very choice design: on one side was depicted a stag, absolutely lifelike, running swiftly, and so well done! On the other side was the portrait of a celebrated General, also an excellent likeness. I cannot describe Vasya's raptures. Meanwhile, time was not being wasted in the parlour. Lizanka went straight up to Arkady Ivanovitch. She took his hand, she thanked him for something, and Arkady Ivanovitch gathered that she was referring to her precious Vasya. Lizanka was, indeed, deeply touched: she had heard that Arkady Ivanovitch was such a true friend of her betrothed, so loved him, so watched over him, guiding him at every step with helpful advice, that she, Lizanka, could hardly help thanking him, could not refrain from feeling grateful, and hoping that Arkady Ivanovitch might like her, if only half as well as Vasya. Then she began questioning him as to whether Vasya was careful of his health, expressed some apprehensions in regard to his marked impulsiveness of character, and his lack of knowledge of men and practical life; she said that she would in time watch over him religiously, that she would take care of and cherish his lot, and finally, she hoped that Arkady Ivanovitch would not leave them, but would live with them.

"We three shall live like one," she cried, with extremely naïve enthusiasm.

But it was time to go. They tried, of course, to keep them, but Vasya answered point blank that it was impossible. Arkady Ivanovitch said the same. The reason was, of course, inquired into, and it came out at once that there was work to be done entrusted to Vasya by Yulian Mastakovitch, urgent, necessary, dreadful work, which must be handed in on the morning of the next day but one, and that it was not only unfinished, but had been completely laid aside. The mamma sighed when she heard of this, while Lizanka was positively scared, and hurried Vasya off in alarm. The last kiss lost nothing from this haste; though brief and hurried it was only the more warm and ardent. At last they parted and the two friends set off home.

Both began at once confiding to each other their impressions as soon as they found themselves in the street. And could they help it? Indeed, Arkady Ivanovitch was in love, desperately in love, with Lizanka. And to whom could he better confide his feelings than to Vasya, the happy man himself. And so he did; he was not bashful, but confessed everything at once to Vasya. Vasya laughed heartily and was immensely delighted, and even observed that this was all that was needed to make them greater friends than ever. "You have guessed my feelings, Vasya," said Arkady Ivanovitch. "Yes, I love her as I love you; she will be my good angel as well as yours, for the radiance of your happiness will be shed on me, too, and I can bask in its warmth. She will keep house for me too, Vasya; my happiness will be in her hands. Let her keep house for me as she will for you. Yes, friendship for you is friendship for her; you are not separable for me now, only I shall have two beings like you instead of one...." Arkady paused in the fullness of his feelings, while Vasya was shaken to the depths of his being by his friend's words. The fact is, he had never expected anything of the sort from Arkady. Arkady Ivanovitch was not very great at talking as a rule, he was not fond of dreaming, either; now he gave way to the liveliest, freshest, rainbow-tinted day-dreams. "How I will protect and cherish you both," he began again. "To begin with, Vasya, I will be godfather to all your children, every one of them; and secondly, Vasya, we must bestir ourselves about the future. We must buy furniture, and take a lodging so that you and she and I can each have a little room to ourselves. Do you know, Vasya, I'll run about to-morrow and look at the notices, on the gates! Three ... no, two rooms, we should not need more. I really believe, Vasya, I talked nonsense this morning, there will be money enough; why, as soon as I glanced into her eyes I calculated at once that there would be enough to live on. It will all be for her. Oh, how we will work! Now, Vasya, we might venture up to twenty-five roubles for rent. A lodging is everything, brother. Nice rooms ... and at once a man is cheerful, and his dreams are of the brightest hues. And, besides, Lizanka will keep the purse for both of us: not a farthing will be wasted. Do you suppose I would go to a restaurant? What do you take me for? Not on any account. And then we shall get a bonus and reward, for we shall be zealous in the service—oh! how we shall work, like oxen toiling in the fields.... Only fancy," and Arkady Ivanovitch's voice was faint with pleasure, "all at once and quite unexpected, twenty-five or thirty roubles.... Whenever there's an extra, there'll be a cap or a scarf or a pair of little stockings. She must knit me a scarf; look what a horrid one I've got, the nasty yellow thing, it did me a bad turn to-day! And you wore a nice one, Vasya, to introduce me while I had my head in a halter.... Though never mind that now. And look here, I undertake all the silver. I am bound to give you some little present,—that will be an honour, that will flatter my vanity.... My bonuses won't fail me, surely; you don't suppose they would give them to Skorohodov? No fear, they won't be landed in that person's pocket. I'll buy you silver spoons, brother, good knives—not silver knives, but thoroughly good ones; and a waistcoat, that is a waistcoat for myself. I shall be best man, of course. Only now, brother, you must keep at it, you must keep at it. I shall stand over you with a stick, brother, to-day and to-morrow and all night; I shall worry you to work. Finish, make haste and finish, brother. And then again to spend the evening, and then again both of us happy; we will go in for loto. We will spend the evening there—oh, it's jolly! Oh, the devil! How, vexing it is I can't help you. I should like to take it and write it all for you.... Why is it our handwriting is not alike?"

"Yes," answered Vasya. "Yes, I must make haste. I think it must be eleven o'clock; we must make haste.... To work!" And saying this, Vasya, who had been all the time alternately smiling and trying to interrupt with some enthusiastic rejoinder the flow of his friend's feelings, and had, in short, been showing the most cordial response, suddenly subsided, sank into silence, and almost ran along the street. It seemed as though some burdensome idea had suddenly chilled his feverish head; he seemed all at once dispirited.

Arkady Ivanovitch felt quite uneasy; he scarcely got an answer to his hurried questions from Vasya, who confined himself to a word or two, sometimes an irrelevant exclamation.

"Why, what is the matter with you, Vasya?" he cried at last, hardly able to keep up with him. "Can you really be so uneasy?"

"Oh, brother, that's enough chatter!" Vasya answered, with vexation.

"Don't be depressed, Vasya—come, come," Arkady interposed. "Why, I have known you write much more in a shorter time! What's the matter? You've simply a talent for it! You can write quickly in an emergency; they are not going to lithograph your copy. You've plenty of time!... The only thing is that you are excited now, and preoccupied, and the work won't go so easily."

Vasya made no reply, or muttered something to himself, and they both ran home in genuine anxiety.

Vasya sat down to the papers at once. Arkady Ivanovitch was quiet and silent; he noiselessly undressed and went to bed, keeping his eyes fixed on Vasya.... A sort of panic came over him.... "What is the matter with him?" he thought to himself, looking at Vasya's face that grew whiter and whiter, at his feverish eyes, at the anxiety that was betrayed in every movement he made, "why, his hand is shaking ... what a stupid! Why did I not advise him to sleep for a couple of hours, till he had slept off his nervous excitement, any way." Vasya had just finished a page, he raised his eyes, glanced casually at Arkady and at once, looking down, took up his pen again.

"Listen, Vasya," Arkady Ivanovitch began suddenly, "wouldn't it be best to sleep a little now? Look, you are in a regular fever."

Vasya glanced at Arkady with vexation, almost with anger, and made no answer.

"Listen, Vasya, you'll make yourself ill."

Vasya at once changed his mind. "How would it be to have tea, Arkady?" he said.

"How so? Why?"

"It will do me good. I am not sleepy, I'm not going to bed! I am going on writing. But now I should like to rest and have a cup of tea, and the worst moment will be over."

"First-rate, brother Vasya, delightful! Just so. I was wanting to propose it myself. And I can't think why it did not occur to me to do so. But I say, Mavra won't get up, she won't wake for anything...."

"True."

"That's no matter, though," cried Arkady Ivanovitch, leaping out of bed. "I will set the samovar myself. It won't be the first time...."

Arkady Ivanovitch ran to the kitchen and set to work to get the samovar; Vasya meanwhile went on writing. Arkady Ivanovitch, moreover, dressed and ran out to the baker's, so that Vasya might have something to sustain him for the night. A quarter of an hour later the samovar was on the table. They began drinking tea, but conversation flagged. Vasya still seemed preoccupied.

"To-morrow," he said at last, as though he had just thought of it, "I shall have to take my congratulations for the New Year...."

"You need not go at all."

"Oh yes, brother, I must," said Vasya.

"Why, I will sign the visitors' book for you everywhere.... How can you? You work to-morrow. You must work to-night, till five o'clock in the morning, as I said, and then get to bed. Or else you will be good for nothing to-morrow. I'll wake you at eight o'clock, punctually."

"But will it be all right, your signing for me?" said Vasya, half assenting.

"Why, what could be better? Everyone does it."

"I am really afraid."

"Why, why?"

"It's all right, you know, with other people, but Yulian Mastakovitch ... he has been so kind to me, you know, Arkasha, and when he notices it's not my own signature——"

"Notices! why, what a fellow you are, really, Vasya! How could he notice?... Come, you know I can imitate your signature awfully well, and make just the same flourish to it, upon my word I can. What nonsense! Who would notice?"

Vasya, made no reply, but emptied his glass hurriedly.... Then he shook his head doubtfully.

"Vasya, dear boy! Ah, if only we succeed! Vasya, what's the matter with you, you quite frighten me! Do you know, Vasya, I am not going to bed now, I am not going to sleep! Show me, have you a great deal left?"

Vasya gave Arkady such a look that his heart sank, and his tongue failed him.

"Vasya, what is the matter? What are you thinking? Why do you look like that?"

"Arkady, I really must go to-morrow to wish Yulian Mastakovitch a happy New Year."

"Well, go then!" said Arkady, gazing at him open-eyed, in uneasy expectation. "I say, Vasya, do write faster; I am advising you for your good, I really am! How often Yulian Mastakovitch himself has said that what he likes particularly about your writing is its legibility. Why, it is all that Skoroplehin cares for, that writing should be good and distinct like a copy, so as afterwards to pocket the paper and take it home for his children to copy; he can't buy copybooks, the blockhead! Yulian Mastakovitch is always saying, always insisting: 'Legible, legible, legible!'... What is the matter? Vasya, I really don't know how to talk to you ... it quite frightens me ... you crush me with your depression."

"It's all right, it's all right," said Vasya, and he fell back in his chair as though fainting. Arkady was alarmed.

"Will you have some water? Vasya! Vasya!"

"Don't, don't," said Vasya, pressing his hand. "I am all right, I only feel sad, I can't tell why. Better talk of something else; let me forget it."

"Calm yourself, for goodness' sake, calm yourself, Vasya. You will finish it all right, on my honour, you will. And even if you don't finish, what will it matter? You talk as though it were a crime!"

"Arkady," said Vasya, looking at his friend with such meaning that Arkady was quite frightened, for Vasya had never been so agitated before.... "If I were alone, as I used to be.... No! I don't mean that. I keep wanting to tell you as a friend, to confide in you.... But why worry you, though?... You see, Arkady, to some much is given, others do a little thing as I do. Well, if gratitude, appreciation, is expected of you ... and you can't give it?"

"Vasya, I don't understand you in the least."

"I have never been ungrateful," Vasya went on softly, as though speaking to himself, "but if I am incapable of expressing all I feel, it seems as though ... it seems, Arkady, as though I am really ungrateful, and that's killing me."

"What next, what next! As though gratitude meant nothing more than your finishing that copy in time? Just think what you are saying, Vasya? Is that the whole expression of gratitude?"

Vasya sank into silence at once, and looked open-eyed at Arkady, as though his unexpected argument had settled all his doubts. He even smiled, but the same melancholy expression came back to his face at once. Arkady, taking this smile as a sign that all his uneasiness was over, and the look that succeeded it as an indication that he was determined to do better, was greatly relieved.

"Well, brother Arkasha, you will wake up," said Vasya, "keep an eye on me; if I fall asleep it will be dreadful. I'll set to work now.... Arkasha?"

"What?"

"Oh, it's nothing, I only ... I meant...."

Vasya settled himself, and said no more, Arkady got into bed. Neither of them said one word about their friends, the Artemyevs. Perhaps both of them felt that they had been a little to blame, and that they ought not to have gone for their jaunt when they did. Arkady soon fell asleep, still worried about Vasya. To his own surprise he woke up exactly at eight o'clock in the morning. Vasya was asleep in his chair with the pen in his hand, pale and exhausted; the candle had burnt out. Mavra was busy getting the samovar ready in the kitchen.

"Vasya, Vasya!" Arkady cried in alarm, "when did you fall asleep?"

Vasya opened his eyes and jumped up from his chair.

"Oh!" he cried, "I must have fallen asleep...."

He flew to the papers—everything was right; all were in order; there was not a blot of ink, nor spot of grease from the candle on them.

"I think I must have fallen asleep about six o'clock," said Vasya. "How cold it is in the night! Let us have tea, and I will go on again...."

"Do you feel better?"

"Yes, yes, I'm all right, I'm all right now."

"A happy New Year to you, brother Vasya."

"And to you too, brother, the same to you, dear boy."

They embraced each other. Vasya's chin was quivering and his eyes were moist. Arkady Ivanovitch was silent, he felt sad. They drank their tea hastily.

"Arkady, I've made up my mind, I am going myself to Yulian Mastakovitch."

"Why, he wouldn't notice——"

"But my conscience feels ill at ease, brother."

"But you know it's for his sake you are sitting here; it's for his sake you are wearing yourself out."

"Enough!"

"Do you know what, brother, I'll go round and see...."

"Whom?" asked Vasya.

"The Artemyevs. I'll take them your good wishes for the New Year as well as mine."

"My dear fellow! Well, I'll stay here; and I see it's a good idea of yours; I shall be working here, I shan't waste my time. Wait one minute, I'll write a note."

"Yes, do brother, do, there's plenty of time. I've still to wash and shave and to brush my best coat. Well, Vasya, we are going to be contented and happy. Embrace me, Vasya."

"Ah, if only we may, brother...."

"Does Mr. Shumkov live here?" they heard a child's voice on the stairs.

"Yes, my dear, yes," said Mavra, showing the visitor in.

"What's that? What is it?" cried Vasya, leaping up from the table and rushing to the entry, "Petinka, you?"

"Good morning, I have the honour to wish you a happy New Year, Vassily Petrovitch," said a pretty boy of ten years old with curly black hair. "Sister sends you her love, and so does Mamma, and Sister told me to give you a kiss for her."

Vasya caught the messenger up in the air and printed a long, enthusiastic kiss on his lips, which were very much like Lizanka's.

"Kiss him, Arkady," he said handing Petya to him, and without touching the ground the boy was transferred to Arkady Ivanovitch's powerful and eager arms.

"Will you have some breakfast, dear?"

"Thank-you, very much. We have had it already, we got up early to-day, the others have gone to church. Sister was two hours curling my hair, and pomading it, washing me and mending my trousers, for I tore them yesterday, playing with Sashka in the street, we were snowballing."

"Well, well, well!"

"So she dressed me up to come and see you, and then pomaded my head and then gave me a regular kissing. She said: 'Go to Vasya, wish him a happy New Year, and ask whether they are happy, whether they had a good night, and ...' to ask something else,—oh yes! whether you had finished the work you spoke of yesterday ... when you were there. Oh, I've got it all written down," said the boy, reading from a slip of paper which he took out of his pocket. "Yes, they were uneasy."

"It will be finished! It will be! Tell her that it will be. I shall finish it, on my word of honour!"

"And something else.... Oh yes, I forgot. Sister sent a little note and a present, and I was forgetting it!..."

"My goodness! Oh, you little darling! Where is it? where is it? That's it, oh! Look, brother, see what she writes. The dar—ling, the precious! You know I saw there yesterday a paper-case for me; it's not finished, so she says, 'I am sending you a lock of my hair, and the other will come later.' Look, brother, look!"

And overwhelmed with rapture he showed Arkady Ivanovitch a curl of luxuriant, jet-black hair; then he kissed it fervently and put it in his breast pocket, nearest his heart.

"Vasya, I shall get you a locket for that curl," Arkady Ivanovitch said resolutely at last.

"And we are going to have hot veal, and to-morrow brains. Mamma wants to make cakes ... but we are not going to have millet porridge," said the boy, after a moment's thought, to wind up his budget of interesting items.

"Oh! what a pretty boy," cried Arkady Ivanovitch. "Vasya, you are the happiest of mortals."

The boy finished his tea, took from Vasya a note, a thousand kisses, and went out happy and frolicsome as before.

"Well, brother," began Arkady Ivanovitch, highly delighted, "you see how splendid it all is; you see. Everything is going well, don't be downcast, don't be uneasy. Go ahead! Get it done, Vasya, get it done. I'll be home at two o'clock. I'll go round to them, and then to Yulian Mastakovitch."

"Well, good-bye, brother; good-bye.... Oh! if only.... Very good, you go, very good," said Vasya, "then I really won't go to Yulian Mastakovitch."

"Good-bye."

"Stay, brother, stay, tell them ... well, whatever you think fit. Kiss her ... and give me a full account of everything afterwards."

"Come, come—of course, I know all about it. This happiness has upset you. The suddenness of it all; you've not been yourself since yesterday. You have not got over the excitement of yesterday. Well, it's settled. Now try and get over it, Vasya. Good-bye, good-bye!"

At last the friends parted. All the morning Arkady Ivanovitch was preoccupied, and could think of nothing but Vasya. He knew his weak, highly nervous character. "Yes, this happiness has upset him, I was right there," he said to himself. "Upon my word, he has made me quite depressed, too, that man will make a tragedy of anything! What a feverish creature! Oh, I must save him! I must save him!" said Arkady, not noticing that he himself was exaggerating into something serious a slight trouble, in reality quite trivial. Only at eleven o'clock he reached the porter's lodge of Yulian Mastakovitch's house, to add his modest name to the long list of illustrious persons who had written their names on a sheet of blotted and scribbled paper in the porter's lodge. What was his surprise when he saw just above his own the signature of Vasya Shumkov! It amazed him. "What's the matter with him?" he thought. Arkady Ivanovitch, who had just been so buoyant with hope, came out feeling upset. There was certainly going to be trouble, but how? And in what form?

He reached the Artemyevs with gloomy forebodings; he seemed absent-minded from the first, and after talking a little with Lizanka went away with tears in his eyes; he was really anxious about Vasya. He went home running, and on the Neva came full tilt upon Vasya himself. The latter, too, was uneasy.

"Where are you going?" cried Arkady Ivanovitch.

Vasya stopped as though he had been caught in a crime.

"Oh, it's nothing, brother, I wanted to go for a walk."

"You could not stand it, and have been to the Artemyevs? Oh, Vasya, Vasya! Why did you go to Yulian Mastakovitch?"

Vasya did not answer, but then with a wave of his hand, he said: "Arkady, I don't know what is the matter with me. I...."

"Come, come, Vasya. I know what it is. Calm yourself. You've been excited, and overwrought ever since yesterday. Only think, it's not much to bear. Everybody's fond of you, everybody's ready to do anything for you; your work is getting on all right; you will get it done, you will certainly get it done. I know that you have been imagining something, you have had apprehensions about something...."

"No, it's all right, it's all right...."

"Do you remember, Vasya, do you remember it was the same with you once before; do you remember, when you got your promotion, in your joy and thankfulness you were so zealous that you spoilt all your work for a week? It is just the same

34

with you now."

"Yes, yes, Arkady; but now it is different, it is not that at all."

"How is it different? And very likely the work is not urgent at all, while you are killing yourself...."

"It's nothing, it's nothing. I am all right, it's nothing. Well, come along!"

"Why, are you going home, and not to them?"

"Yes, brother, how could I have the face to turn up there?... I have changed my mind. It was only that I could not stay on alone without you; now you are coming back with me I'll sit down to write again. Let us go!"

They walked along and for some time were silent. Vasya was in haste.

"Why don't you ask me about them?" said Arkady Ivanovitch.

"Oh, yes! Well, Arkasha, what about them?"

"Vasya, you are not like yourself."

"Oh, I am all right, I am all right. Tell me everything, Arkasha," said Vasya, in an imploring voice, as though to avoid further explanations. Arkady Ivanovitch sighed. He felt utterly at a loss, looking at Vasya.

His account of their friends roused Vasya. He even grew talkative. They had dinner together. Lizanka's mother had filled Arkady Ivanovitch's pockets with little cakes, and eating them the friends grew more cheerful. After dinner Vasya promised to take a nap, so as to sit up all night. He did, in fact, lie down. In the morning, some one whom it was impossible to refuse had invited Arkady Ivanovitch to tea. The friends parted. Arkady promised to come back as soon as he could, by eight o'clock if possible. The three hours of separation seemed to him like three years. At last he got away and rushed back to Vasya. When he went into the room, he found it in darkness. Vasya was not at home. He asked Mavra. Mavra said that he had been writing all the time, and had not slept at all, then he had paced up and down the room, and after that, an hour before, he had run out, saying he would be back in half-an-hour; "and when, says he, Arkady Ivanovitch comes in, tell him, old woman, says he," Mavra told him in conclusion, "that I have gone out for a walk," and he repeated the order three or four times.

"He is at the Artemyevs," thought Arkady Ivanovitch, and he shook his head.

A minute later he jumped up with renewed hope.

"He has simply finished," he thought, "that's all it is; he couldn't wait, but ran off there. But, no! he would have waited for me.... Let's have a peep what he has there."

He lighted a candle, and ran to Vasya's writing-table: the work had made progress and it looked as though there were not much left to do. Arkady Ivanovitch was about to investigate further, when Vasya himself walked in....

"Oh, you are here?" he cried, with a start of dismay.

Arkady Ivanovitch was silent. He was afraid to question Vasya. The latter dropped his eyes and remained silent too, as he began sorting the papers. At last their eyes met. The look in Vasya's was so beseeching, imploring, and broken, that Arkady shuddered when he saw it. His heart quivered and was full.

"Vasya, my dear boy, what is it? What's wrong?" he cried, rushing to him and squeezing him in his arms. "Explain to me, I don't understand you, and your depression. What is the matter with you, my poor, tormented boy? What is it? Tell me all about it, without hiding anything. It can't be only this——"

Vasya held him tight and could say nothing. He could scarcely breathe.

"Don't, Vasya, don't! Well, if you don't finish it, what then? I don't understand you; tell me your trouble. You see it is for your sake I.... Oh dear! oh dear!" he said, walking up and down the room and clutching at everything he came across, as though seeking at once some remedy for Vasya. "I will go to Yulian Mastakovitch instead of you to-morrow. I will ask him—entreat him—to let you have another day. I will explain it all to him, anything, if it worries you so...."

"God forbid!" cried Vasya, and turned as white as the wall. He could scarcely stand on his feet.

"Vasya! Vasya!"

Vasya pulled himself together. His lips were quivering; he tried to say something, but could only convulsively squeeze Arkady's hand in silence. His hand was cold. Arkady stood facing him, full of anxious and miserable suspense. Vasya raised his eyes again.

"Vasya, God bless you, Vasya! You wring my heart, my dear boy, my friend."

Tears gushed from Vasya's eyes; he flung himself on Arkady's bosom.

"I have deceived you, Arkady," he said. "I have deceived you. Forgive me, forgive me! I have been faithless to your friendship...."

"What is it, Vasya? What is the matter?" asked Arkady, in real alarm.

"Look!"

And with a gesture of despair Vasya tossed out of the drawer on to the table six thick manuscripts, similar to the one he had copied.

"What's this?"

"What I have to get through by the day after to-morrow. I haven't done a quarter! Don't ask me, don't ask me how it has happened," Vasya went on, speaking at once of what was distressing him so terribly. "Arkady, dear friend, I don't know myself what came over me. I feel as though I were coming out of a dream. I have wasted three weeks doing nothing. I kept ... I ... kept going to see her.... My heart was aching, I was tormented by ... the uncertainty ... I could not write. I did not even think about it. Only now, when happiness is at hand for me, I have come to my senses."

"Vasya," began Arkady Ivanovitch resolutely, "Vasya, I will save you. I understand it all. It's a serious matter; I will save you. Listen! listen to me: I will go to Yulian Mastakovitch to-morrow.... Don't shake your head; no, listen! I will tell him exactly how it has all been; let me do that ... I will explain to him.... I will go into everything. I will tell him how crushed you are, how you are worrying yourself."

"Do you know that you are killing me now?" Vasya brought out, turning cold with horror.

Arkady Ivanovitch turned pale, but at once controlling himself, laughed.

"Is that all? Is that all?" he said. "Upon my word, Vasya, upon my word! Aren't you ashamed? Come, listen! I see that I am grieving you. You see I understand you; I know what is passing in your heart. Why, we have been living together for five years, thank God! You are such a kind, soft-hearted fellow, but weak, unpardonably weak. Why, even Lizaveta Mikalovna has noticed it. And you are a dreamer, and that's a bad thing, too; you may go from bad to worse, brother. I tell you, I know what you want! You would like Yulian Mastakovitch, for instance, to be beside himself and, maybe, to give a ball, too, from joy, because you are going to get married.... Stop, stop! you are frowning. You see that at one word from me you are offended on Yulian Mastakovitch's account. I'll let him alone. You know I respect him just as much as you do. But argue as you may, you can't prevent my thinking that you would like there to be no one unhappy in the whole world when you are getting married.... Yes, brother, you must admit that you would like me, for instance, your best friend, to come in for a fortune of a hundred thousand all of a sudden, you would like all the enemies in the world to be suddenly, for no rhyme or reason, reconciled, so that in their joy they might all embrace one another in the middle of the street, and then, perhaps, come here to call on you. Vasya, my dear boy, I am not laughing; it is true; you've said as much to me long ago, in different ways. Because you are happy, you want every one, absolutely every one, to become happy at once. It hurts you and troubles you to be happy alone. And so you want at once to do your utmost to be worthy of that happiness, and maybe to do some great deed to satisfy your conscience. Oh! I understand how ready you are to distress yourself for having suddenly been remiss just where you ought to have shown your zeal, your capacity ... well, maybe your gratitude, as you say. It is very bitter for you to think that Yulian

Mastakovitch may frown and even be angry when he sees that you have not justified the expectations he had of you. It hurts you to think that you may hear reproaches from the man you look upon as your benefactor—and at such a moment! when your heart is full of joy and you don't know on whom to lavish your gratitude.... Isn't that true? It is, isn't it?"

Arkady Ivanovitch, whose voice was trembling, paused, and drew a deep breath.

Vasya looked affectionately at his friend. A smile passed over his lips. His face even lighted up, as though with a gleam of hope.

"Well, listen, then," Arkady Ivanovitch began again, growing more hopeful, "there's no necessity that you should forfeit Yulian Mastakovitch's favour.... Is there, dear boy? Is there any question of it? And since it is so," said Arkady, jumping up, "I shall sacrifice myself for you. I am going to-morrow to Yulian Mastakovitch, and don't oppose me. You magnify your failure to a crime, Vasya. Yulian Mastakovitch is magnanimous and merciful, and, what is more, he is not like you. He will listen to you and me, and get us out of our trouble, brother Vasya. Well, are you calmer?"

Vasya pressed his friend's hands with tears in his eyes.

"Hush, hush, Arkady," he said, "the thing is settled. I haven't finished, so very well; if I haven't finished, I haven't finished, and there's no need for you to go. I will tell him all about it, I will go myself. I am calmer now, I am perfectly calm; only you mustn't go.... But listen...."

"Vasya, my dear boy," Arkady Ivanovitch cried joyfully, "I judged from what you said. I am glad that you have thought better of things and have recovered yourself. But whatever may befall you, whatever happens, I am with you, remember that. I see that it worries you to think of my speaking to Yulian Mastakovitch— and I won't say a word, not a word, you shall tell him yourself. You see, you shall go to-morrow.... Oh no, you had better not go, you'll go on writing here, you see, and I'll find out about this work, whether it is very urgent or not, whether it must be done by the time or not, and if you don't finish it in time what will come of it. Then I will run back to you. Do you see, do you see! There is still hope; suppose the work is not urgent—it may be all right. Yulian Mastakovitch may not remember, then all is saved."

Vasya shook his head doubtfully. But his grateful eyes never left his friend's face.

"Come, that's enough, I am so weak, so tired," he said, sighing. "I don't want to think about it. Let us talk of something else. I won't write either now; do you know I'll only finish two short pages just to get to the end of a passage. Listen ... I have long wanted to ask you, how is it you know me so well?"

Tears dropped from Vasya's eyes on Arkady's hand.

"If you knew, Vasya, how fond I am of you, you would not ask that—yes!"

"Yes, yes, Arkady, I don't know that, because I don't know why you are so fond of me. Yes, Arkady, do you know, even your love has been killing me? Do you know, ever so many times, particularly when I am thinking of you in bed (for I always think of you when I am falling asleep), I shed tears, and my heart throbs at the thought ... at the thought.... Well, at the thought that you are so fond of me, while I can do nothing to relieve my heart, can do nothing to repay you."

"You see, Vasya, you see what a fellow you are! Why, how upset you are now," said Arkady, whose heart ached at that moment and who remembered the scene in the street the day before.

"Nonsense, you want me to be calm, but I never have been so calm and happy! Do you know.... Listen, I want to tell you all about it, but I am afraid of wounding you.... You keep scolding me and being vexed; and I am afraid.... See how I am trembling now, I don't know why. You see, this is what I want to say. I feel as though I had never known myself before—yes! Yes, I only began to understand other people too, yesterday. I did not feel or appreciate things fully, brother. My heart ... was hard.... Listen how has it happened, that I have never done good to any one, any one in the world, because I couldn't—I am not even pleasant to look at.... But everybody does me good! You, to begin with: do you suppose I don't see that? Only I said nothing; only I said nothing."

"Hush, Vasya!"

"Oh, Arkasha! ... it's all right," Vasya interrupted, hardly able to articulate for tears. "I talked to you yesterday about Yulian Mastakovitch. And you know yourself how stern and severe he is, even you have come in for a reprimand from him; yet he deigned to jest with me yesterday, to show his affection, and kind-heartedness, which he prudently conceals from every one...."

"Come, Vasya, that only shows you deserve your good fortune."

"Oh, Arkasha! How I longed to finish all this.... No, I shall ruin my good luck! I feel that! Oh no, not through that," Vasya added, seeing that Arkady glanced at the heap of urgent work lying on the table, "that's nothing, that's only paper covered with writing ... it's nonsense! That matter's settled.... I went to see them to-day, Arkasha; I did not go in. I felt depressed and sad. I simply stood at the door. She was playing the piano, I listened. You see, Arkady," he went on, dropping his voice, "I did not dare to go in."

"I say, Vasya—what is the matter with you? You look at one so strangely."

"Oh, it's nothing, I feel a little sick; my legs are trembling; it's because I sat up last night. Yes! Everything looks green before my eyes. It's here, here——"

He pointed to his heart. He fainted. When he came to himself Arkady tried to take forcible measures. He tried to compel him to go to bed. Nothing would induce Vasya to consent. He shed tears, wrung his hands, wanted to write, was absolutely set on finishing his two pages. To avoid exciting him Arkady let him sit down to the work.

"Do you know," said Vasya, as he settled himself in his place, "an idea has occurred to me? There is hope."

He smiled to Arkady, and his pale face lighted up with a gleam of hope.

"I will take him what is done the day after to-morrow. About the rest I will tell a lie. I will say it has been burnt, that it has been sopped in water, that I have lost it.... That, in fact, I have not finished it; I cannot lie. I will explain, do you know, what? I'll explain to him all about it. I will tell him how it was that I could not. I'll tell him about my love; he has got married himself just lately, he'll understand me. I will do it all, of course, respectfully, quietly; he will see my tears and be touched by them...."

"Yes, of course, you must go, you must go and explain to him.... But there's no need of tears! Tears for what? Really, Vasya, you quite scare me."

"Yes, I'll go, I'll go. But now let me write, let me write, Arkasha. I am not interfering with any one, let me write!"

Arkady flung himself on the bed. He had no confidence in Vasya, no confidence at all. "Vasya was capable of anything, but to ask forgiveness for what? how? That was not the point. The point was, that Vasya had not carried out his obligations, that Vasya felt guilty *in his own eyes*, felt that he was ungrateful to destiny, that Vasya was crushed, overwhelmed by happiness and thought himself unworthy of it; that, in fact, he was simply trying to find an excuse to go off his head on that point, and that he had not recovered from the unexpectedness of what had happened the day before; that's what it is," thought Arkady Ivanovitch. "I must save him. I must reconcile him to himself. He will be his own ruin." He thought and thought, and resolved to go at once next day to Yulian Mastakovitch, and to tell him all about it.

Vasya was sitting writing. Arkady Ivanovitch, worn out, lay down to think things over again, and only woke at daybreak.

"Damnation! Again!" he cried, looking at Vasya; the latter was still sitting writing.

Arkady rushed up to him, seized him and forcibly put him to bed. Vasya was smiling: his eyes were closing with sleep. He could hardly speak.

"I wanted to go to bed," he said. "Do you know, Arkady, I have an idea; I shall finish. I made my pen go faster! I could not have sat at it any longer; wake me at eight o'clock."

Without finishing his sentence, he dropped asleep and slept like the dead.

"Mavra," said Arkady Ivanovitch to Mavra, who came in with the tea, "he asked to be waked in an hour. Don't wake him on any account! Let him sleep ten hours, if he can. Do you understand?"

"I understand, sir."

"Don't get the dinner, don't bring in the wood, don't make a noise or it will be the worse for you. If he asks for me, tell him I have gone to the office—do you understand?"

"I understand, bless you, sir; let him sleep and welcome! I am glad my gentlemen should sleep well, and I take good care of their things. And about that cup that was broken, and you blamed me, your honour, it wasn't me, it was poor pussy broke it, I ought to have kept an eye on her. 'S-sh, you confounded thing,' I said."

"Hush, be quiet, be quiet!"

Arkady Ivanovitch followed Mavra out into the kitchen, asked for the key and locked her up there. Then he went to the office. On the way he considered how he could present himself before Yulian Mastakovitch, and whether it would be appropriate and not impertinent. He went into the office timidly, and timidly inquired whether His Excellency were there; receiving the answer that he was not and would not be, Arkady Ivanovitch instantly thought of going to his flat, but reflected very prudently that if Yulian Mastakovitch had not come to the office he would certainly be busy at home. He remained. The hours seemed to him endless. Indirectly he inquired about the work entrusted to Shumkov, but no one knew anything about this. All that was known was that Yulian Mastakovitch did employ him on special jobs, but what they were—no one could say. At last it struck three o'clock, and Arkady Ivanovitch rushed out, eager to get home. In the vestibule he was met by a clerk, who told him that Vassily Petrovitch Shumkov had come about one o'clock and asked, the clerk added, "whether you were here, and whether Yulian Mastakovitch had been here." Hearing this Arkady Ivanovitch took a sledge and hastened home beside himself with alarm.

Shumkov was at home. He was walking about the room in violent excitement. Glancing at Arkady Ivanovitch, he immediately controlled himself, reflected, and hastened to conceal his emotion. He sat down to his papers without a word. He seemed to avoid his friend's questions, seemed to be bothered by them, to be pondering to himself on some plan, and deciding to conceal his decision, because he could not reckon further on his friend's affection. This struck Arkady, and his heart ached with a poignant and oppressive pain. He sat on the bed and began turning over the leaves of some book, the only one he had in his possession, keeping his eye on poor Vasya. But Vasya remained obstinately silent, writing, and not raising his head. So passed several hours, and Arkady's misery reached an extreme point. At last, at eleven o'clock, Vasya lifted his head and looked with a fixed, vacant stare at Arkady. Arkady waited. Two or three minutes passed; Vasya did not speak.

"Vasya!" cried Arkady.

Vasya made no answer.

"Vasya!" he repeated, jumping up from the bed, "Vasya, what is the matter with you? What is it?" he cried, running up to him.

Vasya raised his eyes and again looked at him with the same vacant, fixed stare.

"He's in a trance!" thought Arkady, trembling all over with fear. He seized a bottle of water, raised Vasya, poured some water on his head, moistened his temples, rubbed his hands in his own— and Vasya came to himself. "Vasya, Vasya!" cried Arkady, unable to restrain his tears. "Vasya, save yourself, rouse yourself, rouse yourself!..." He could say no more, but held him tight in his arms. A look as of some oppressive sensation passed over Vasya's face; he rubbed his forehead and clutched at his head, as though he were afraid it would burst.

"I don't know what is the matter with me," he added, at last. "I feel torn to pieces. Come, it's all right, it's all right! Give over, Arkady; don't grieve," he repeated, looking at him with sad, exhausted eyes. "Why be so anxious? Come!"

"You, you comforting me!" cried Arkady, whose heart was torn. "Vasya," he said at last, "lie down and have a little nap, won't you? Don't wear yourself out for nothing! You'll set to work better afterwards."

"Yes, yes," said Vasya, "by all means, I'll lie down, very good. Yes! you see I meant to finish, but now I've changed my mind, yes...."

And Arkady led him to the bed.

"Listen, Vasya," he said firmly, "we must settle this matter finally. Tell me what were you thinking about?"

"Oh!" said Vasya, with a flourish of his weak hand turning over on the other side.

"Come, Vasya, come, make up your mind. I don't want to hurt you. I can't be silent any longer. You won't sleep till you've made up your mind, I know."

"As you like, as you like," Vasya repeated enigmatically.

"He will give in," thought Arkady Ivanovitch.

"Attend to me, Vasya," he said, "remember what I say, and I will save you to-morrow; to-morrow I will decide your fate! What am I saying, your fate? You have so frightened me, Vasya, that I am using your own words. Fate, indeed! It's simply nonsense, rubbish! You don't want to lose Yulian Mastakovitch's favour—affection, if you like. No! And you won't lose it, you will see. I——"

Arkady Ivanovitch would have said more, but Vasya interrupted him. He sat up in bed, put both arms round Arkady Ivanovitch's neck and kissed him.

"Enough," he said in a weak voice, "enough! Say no more about that!"

And again he turned his face to the wall.

"My goodness!" thought Arkady, "my goodness! What is the matter with him? He is utterly lost. What has he in his mind! He will be his own undoing."

Arkady looked at him in despair.

"If he were to fall ill," thought Arkady, "perhaps it would be better. His trouble would pass off with illness, and that might be the best way of settling the whole business. But what nonsense I am talking. Oh, my God!"

Meanwhile Vasya seemed to be asleep. Arkady Ivanovitch was relieved. "A good sign," he thought. He made up his mind to sit beside him all night. But Vasya was restless; he kept twitching and tossing about on the bed, and opening his eyes for an instant. At last exhaustion got the upper hand, he slept like the dead. It was about two o'clock in the morning, Arkady Ivanovitch began to doze in the chair with his elbow on the table!

He had a strange and agitated dream. He kept fancying that he was not asleep, and that Vasya was still lying on the bed. But strange to say, he fancied that Vasya was pretending, that he was deceiving him, that he was getting up, stealthily watching him out of the corner of his eye, and was stealing up to the writing table. Arkady felt a scalding pain at his heart; he felt vexed and sad and oppressed to see Vasya not trusting him, hiding and concealing himself from him. He tried to catch hold of him, to call out, to carry him to the bed. Then Vasya kept shrieking in his arms, and he laid on the bed a lifeless corpse. He opened his eyes and woke up; Vasya was sitting before him at the table, writing.

Hardly able to believe his senses, Arkady glanced at the bed; Vasya was not there. Arkady jumped up in a panic, still under the influence of his dream. Vasya did not stir; he went on writing. All at once Arkady noticed with horror that Vasya was moving a dry pen over the paper, was turning over perfectly blank pages, and hurrying, hurrying to fill up the paper as though he were doing his work in a most thorough and efficient way. "No, this is not a trance," thought Arkady Ivanovitch, and he trembled all over.

"Vasya, Vasya, speak to me," he cried, clutching him by the shoulder. But Vasya did not speak; he went on as before, scribbling with a dry pen over the paper.

"At last I have made the pen go faster," he said, without looking up at Arkady.

Arkady seized his hand and snatched away the pen.

A moan broke from Vasya. He dropped his hand and raised his eyes to Arkady; then with an air of misery and exhaustion he passed his hand over his forehead as though he wanted to shake off some leaden weight that was pressing upon his whole being, and slowly, as though lost in thought, he let his head sink on his breast.

"Vasya, Vasya!" cried Arkady in despair. "Vasya!"

A minute later Vasya looked at him, tears stood in his large blue eyes, and his pale, mild face wore a look of infinite suffering. He whispered something.

"What, what is it?" cried Arkady, bending down to him.

"What for, why are they doing it to me?" whispered Vasya. "What for? What have I done?"

"Vasya, what is it? What are you afraid of? What is it?" cried Arkady, wringing his hands in despair.

"Why are they sending me for a soldier?" said Vasya, looking his friend straight in the face. "Why is it? What have I done?"

Arkady's hair stood on end with horror; he refused to believe his ears. He stood over him, half dead.

A minute later he pulled himself together. "It's nothing, it's only for the minute," he said to himself, with pale face and blue, quivering lips, and he hastened to put on his outdoor things. He meant to run straight for a doctor. All at once Vasya called to him. Arkady rushed to him and clasped him in his arms like a mother whose child is being torn from her.

"Arkady, Arkady, don't tell any one! Don't tell any one, do you hear? It is my trouble, I must bear it alone."

"What is it—what is it? Rouse yourself, Vasya, rouse yourself!"

Vasya sighed, and slow tears trickled down his cheeks.

"Why kill her? How is she to blame?" he muttered in an agonized, heartrending voice. "The sin is mine, the sin is mine!"

He was silent for a moment.

"Farewell, my love! Farewell, my love!" he whispered, shaking his luckless head. Arkady started, pulled himself together and would have rushed for the doctor. "Let us go, it is time," cried Vasya, carried away by Arkady's last movement. "Let us go, brother, let us go; I am ready. You lead the way." He paused and looked at Arkady with a downcast and mistrustful face.

"Vasya, for goodness' sake, don't follow me! Wait for me here. I will come back to you directly, directly," said Arkady Ivanovitch, losing his head and snatching up his cap to run for a doctor. Vasya sat down at once, he was quiet and docile; but there was a gleam of some desperate resolution in his eye. Arkady turned back, snatched up from the table an open penknife, looked at the poor fellow for the last time, and ran out of the flat.

It was eight o'clock. It had been broad daylight for some time in the room.

He found no one. He was running about for a full hour. All the doctors whose addresses he had got from the house porter when he inquired of the latter whether there were no doctor living in the building, had gone out, either to their work or on their private affairs. There was one who saw patients. This one questioned at length and in detail the servant who announced that Nefedevitch had called, asking him who it was, from whom he came, what was the matter, and concluded by saying that he could not go, that he had a great deal to do, and that patients of that kind ought to be taken to a hospital.

Then Arkady, exhausted, agitated, and utterly taken aback by this turn of affairs, cursed all the doctors on earth, and rushed home in the utmost alarm about Vasya. He ran into the flat. Mavra, as though there were nothing the matter, went on scrubbing the floor, breaking up wood and preparing to light the stove. He went into the room; there was no trace of Vasya, he had gone out.

"Which way? Where? Where will the poor fellow be off to?" thought Arkady, frozen with terror. He began questioning Mavra. She knew nothing, had neither seen nor heard him go out, God bless him! Nefedevitch rushed off to the Artemyevs'.

It occurred to him for some reason that he must be there.

It was ten o'clock by the time he arrived. They did not expect him, knew nothing and had heard nothing. He stood before them frightened, distressed, and asked where was Vasya? The mother's legs gave way under her; she sank back on the sofa. Lizanka, trembling with alarm, began asking what had happened. What could he say? Arkady Ivanovitch got out of it as best he could, invented some tale which of course was not believed, and fled, leaving them distressed and anxious. He flew to his department that he might not be too late there, and he let them know that steps might be taken at once. On the way it occurred to him that Vasya would be at Yulian Mastakovitch's. That was more likely than anything: Arkady had thought of that first of all, even before the Artemyevs'. As he drove by His Excellency's door, he thought of stopping, but at once told the driver to go straight on. He made up his mind to try and find out whether anything had happened at the office, and if he were not there to go to His Excellency, ostensibly to report on Vasya. Some one must be informed of it.

As soon as he got into the waiting-room he was surrounded by fellow-clerks, for the most part young men of his own standing in the service. With one voice they began asking him what had happened to Vasya? At the same time they all told him that Vasya had gone out of his mind, and thought that he was to be sent for a soldier as a punishment for having neglected his work. Arkady Ivanovitch, answering them in all directions, or rather avoiding giving a direct answer to any one, rushed into the inner room. On the way he learned that Vasya was in Yulian Mastakovitch's private room, that every one had been there and that Esper Ivanovitch had gone in there too. He was stopped on the way. One of the senior clerks asked him who he was and what he wanted? Without distinguishing the person he said something about Vasya and went straight into the room. He heard Yulian Mastakovitch's voice from within. "Where are you going?" some one asked him at the very door. Arkady Ivanovitch was almost in despair; he was on the point of turning back, but through the open door he saw his poor Vasya. He pushed the door and squeezed his way into the room. Every one seemed to be in confusion and perplexity, because Yulian Mastakovitch was apparently much chagrined. All the more important personages were standing about him talking, and coming to no decision. At a little distance stood Vasya. Arkady's heart sank when he looked at him. Vasya was standing, pale, with his head up, stiffly erect, like a recruit before a new officer, with his feet together and his hands held rigidly at his sides. He was looking Yulian Mastakovitch straight in the face. Arkady was noticed at once, and some one who knew that they lodged together mentioned the fact to His Excellency. Arkady was led up to him. He tried to make some answer to the questions put to him, glanced at Yulian Mastakovitch and seeing on his face a look of genuine compassion, began trembling and sobbing like a child. He even did more, he snatched His Excellency's hand and held it to his eyes, wetting it with his tears, so that Yulian Mastakovitch was obliged to draw it hastily away, and waving it in the air, said, "Come, my dear fellow, come! I see you have a good heart." Arkady sobbed and turned an imploring look on every one. It seemed to him that they were all brothers of his dear Vasya, that they were all worried and weeping about him. "How, how has it happened? how has it happened?" asked Yulian Mastakovitch. "What has sent him out of his mind?"

"Gra—gra—gratitude!" was all Arkady Ivanovitch could articulate.

Every one heard his answer with amazement, and it seemed strange and incredible to every one that a man could go out of his mind from gratitude. Arkady explained as best he could.

"Good Heavens! what a pity!" said Yulian Mastakovitch at last. "And the work entrusted to him was not important, and not urgent in the least. It was not worth while for a man to kill himself over it! Well, take him away!"... At this point Yulian Mastakovitch turned to Arkady Ivanovitch again, and began questioning him once more. "He begs," he said, pointing to Vasya, "that some girl should not be told of this. Who is she—his betrothed, I suppose?"

Arkady began to explain. Meanwhile Vasya seemed to be thinking of something, as though he were straining his memory to the utmost to recall some important, necessary matter, which was particularly wanted at this moment. From time to time he looked round with a distressed face, as though hoping some one would remind him of what he had forgotten. He fastened his eyes on Arkady. All of a sudden there was a gleam of hope in his eyes; he moved with the left leg forward, took three steps as smartly as he could, clicking with his right boot as soldiers do when they move forward at the call from their officer. Every one was waiting to see what would happen.

"I have a physical defect and am small and weak, and I am not fit for military service, Your Excellency," he said abruptly.

At that every one in the room felt a pang at his heart, and firm as was Yulian Mastakovitch's character, tears trickled from his eyes.

"Take him away," he said, with a wave of his hands.

"Present!" said Vasya in an undertone; he wheeled round to the left and marched out of the room. All who were interested in his fate followed him out. Arkady pushed his way out behind the others. They made Vasya sit down in the waiting-room till the carriage came which had been ordered to take him to the hospital. He sat down in silence and seemed in great anxiety. He nodded to any one he recognized as though saying good-bye. He looked round towards the door every minute, and prepared himself to set off when he should be told it was time. People crowded in a close circle round him; they were all shaking their heads and lamenting. Many of them were much impressed by his story, which had suddenly become known. Some discussed his illness, while others expressed their pity and high opinion of Vasya, saying that he was such a quiet, modest young man, that he had been so promising; people described what efforts he had made to learn, how eager he was for knowledge, how he had worked to educate himself. "He had risen by his own efforts from a humble position," some one observed. They spoke with emotion of His Excellency's affection for him. Some of them fell to explaining why Vasya was possessed by the idea that he was being sent for a soldier, because he had not finished his work. They said that the poor fellow had so lately belonged to the class liable for military service and had only received his first grade through the good offices of Yulian Mastakovitch, who had had the cleverness to discover his talent, his docility, and the rare mildness of his disposition. In fact, there was a great number of views and theories.

A very short fellow-clerk of Vasya's was conspicuous as being particularly distressed. He was not very young, probably about thirty. He was pale as a sheet, trembling all over and smiling queerly, perhaps because any scandalous affair or terrible scene both frightens, and at the same time somewhat rejoices the outside spectator. He kept running round the circle that surrounded Vasya, and as he was so short, stood on tiptoe and caught at the button of every one—that is, of those with whom he felt entitled to take such a liberty—and kept saying that he knew how it had all happened, that it was not so simple, but a very important matter, that it couldn't be left without further inquiry; then stood on tiptoe again, whispered in some one's ear, nodded his head again two or three times, and ran round again. At last everything was over. The porter made his appearance, and an attendant from the hospital went up to Vasya and told him it was time to start. Vasya jumped up in a flutter and went with them, looking about him. He was looking about for some one.

"Vasya, Vasya!" cried Arkady Ivanovitch, sobbing. Vasya stopped, and Arkady squeezed his way up to him. They flung themselves into each other's arms in a last bitter embrace. It was sad to see them. What monstrous calamity was wringing the tears from their eyes! What were they weeping for? What was their trouble? Why did they not understand one another?

"Here, here, take it! Take care of it," said Shumkov, thrusting a paper of some kind into Arkady's hand. "They will take it away from me. Bring it me later on; bring it ... take care of it...." Vasya could not finish, they called to him. He ran hurriedly downstairs, nodding to every one, saying good-bye to every one. There was despair in his face. At last he was put in the carriage and taken away. Arkady made haste to open the paper: it was Liza's curl of black hair, from which Vasya had never parted. Hot tears gushed from Arkady's eyes: oh, poor Liza!

When office hours were over, he went to the Artemyevs'. There is no need to describe what happened there! Even Petya, little Petya, though he could not quite understand what had happened to dear Vasya, went into a corner, hid his face in his little hands, and sobbed in the fullness of his childish heart. It was quite dusk when Arkady returned home. When he reached the Neva he stood still for a minute and turned a keen glance up the river into the smoky frozen thickness of the distance, which was suddenly flushed crimson with the last purple and blood-red glow of sunset, still smouldering on the misty horizon.... Night lay over the city, and the wide plain of the Neva, swollen with frozen snow, was shining in the last gleams of the sun with myriads of sparks of gleaming hoar frost. There was a frost of twenty degrees. A cloud of frozen steam hung about the overdriven horses and the hurrying people. The condensed atmosphere quivered at the slightest sound, and from all the roofs on both sides of the river, columns of smoke rose up like giants and floated across the cold sky, intertwining and untwining as they went, so that it seemed new buildings were rising up above the old, a new town was taking shape in the air.... It seemed as if all that world, with all its inhabitants, strong and weak, with all their habitations, the refuges of the poor, or the gilded palaces for the comfort of the powerful of this world was at that twilight hour like a fantastic vision of fairy-land, like a dream which in its turn would vanish and pass away like vapour into the dark blue sky. A strange thought came to poor Vasya's forlorn friend. He started, and his heart seemed at that instant flooded with a hot rush of blood kindled by a powerful, overwhelming sensation he had never known before. He seemed only now to understand all the trouble, and to know why his poor Vasya had gone out of his mind, unable to bear his happiness. His lips twitched, his eyes lighted up, he turned pale, and as it were had a clear vision into something new.

He became gloomy and depressed, and lost all his gaiety. His old lodging grew hateful to him—he took a new room. He did not care to visit the Artemyevs, and indeed he could not. Two years later he met Lizanka in church. She was by then married; beside her walked a wet nurse with a tiny baby. They greeted each other, and for a long time avoided all mention of the past. Liza said that, thank God, she was happy, that she was not badly off, that her husband was a kind man and that she was fond of him.... But suddenly in the middle of a sentence her eyes filled with tears, her voice failed, she turned away, and bowed down to the church pavement to hide her grief.